This book belongs to:

_____

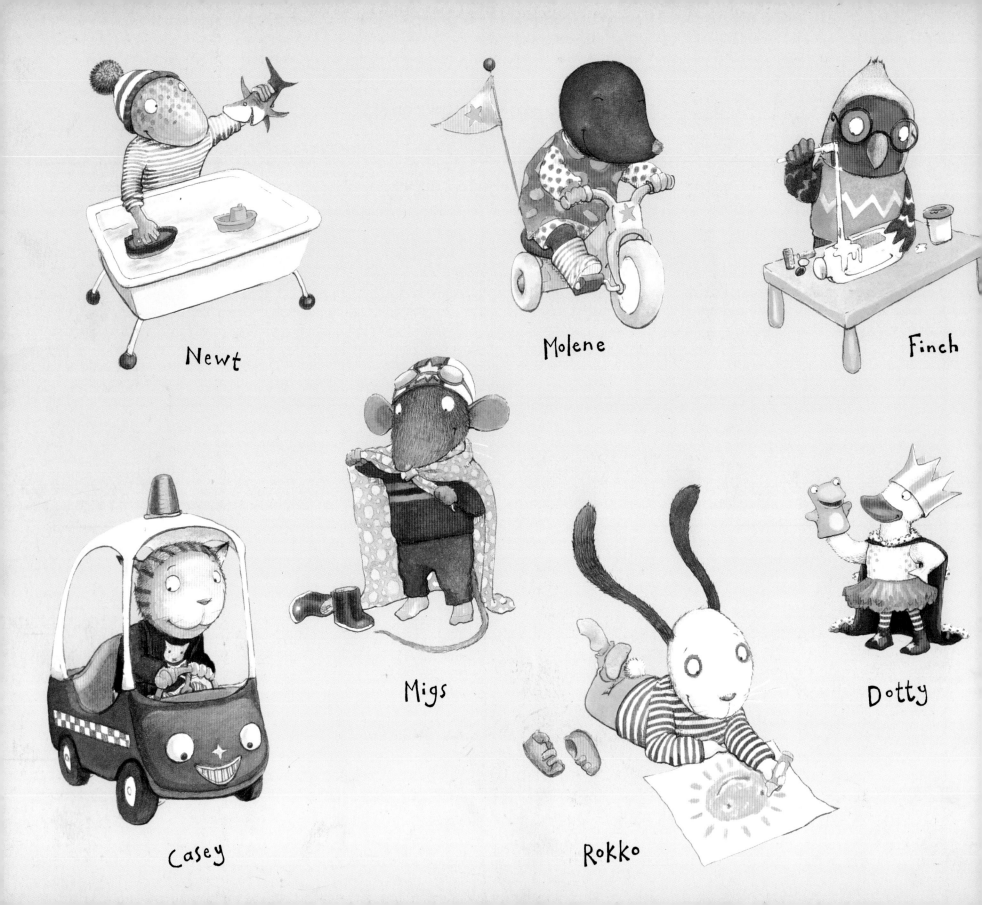

Newt

Molene

Finch

Migs

Casey

Rokko

Dotty

Casey

Dotty

Newt

Finch

Migs

Molene

Rokko

For Elizabeth Hodgkinson

This paperback edition first published in 2015 by Andersen Press Ltd.
First published in Great Britain in 2014 by Andersen Press Ltd.,
20 Vauxhall Bridge Road, London SW1V 2SA.

Copyright © Jo Hodgkinson, 2014.

The rights of Jo Hodgkinson to be identified as the author and
illustrator of this work have been asserted by her in accordance
with the Copyright, Designs and Patents Act, 1988.
All rights reserved.

Printed and bound in Malaysia by Tien Wah Press.

1 3 5 7 9 10 8 6 4 2

British Library Cataloguing in Publication Data available.

TOYS

"Come on, Migs," calls out his Mum,
"Starting school's fantastic fun!"

She hugs him tight, she waves goodbye.
Migs is trying not to cry.

The teacher says, "Let's learn some names. Mine's Miss Doodle," she explains.

Then everyone takes turns to speak.   Migs holds his breath and whispers, "Squeak."

He watches all the fun and sighs,
"I wish I wasn't quite so shy."

He finds a hat,

a cloak, some boots.

He feels so brave in this new suit.

"I'm MIGHTY MIGS and I declare

that I'm as strong as any bear!
I'm not a shy mouse any more!

I'm like a lion,
hear me ROAR!
I'm Mighty Migs. Just look and see,
no train can move as fast as me!"

"Please, slow down, Migs!"

Miss Doodle calls.

"That cloak's too long!
You'll trip and fall."

"I'm Mighty Migs,
no need to fear!

A bit of tape stuck over here,

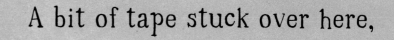

"Stop!" Rokko says. "It's not the same.
It looked so nice before you came."

Through tears he says, "Migs, go away!
I'd rather that you didn't stay."

Migs looks to find a place to hide,
he sees a box and climbs inside.

Migs sits and thinks. At last it's clear
"Miss Doodle, I've a great idea!"
Miss Doodle claps, "I'll call the team.
This plan's a winner, what a scheme!"

Soon everyone does what they can
to help Migs with his **super plan.**

"SSHH!" whispers Migs. "I'll take a look...
He's in the corner with a book."

They sound the fanfare, Rokko squeals,
"My **boat!** I can't believe it's real."
Migs says, "We made it just for you."
Says Rokko, "Look, there's room for two."

They take positions,

read the map.

Sail round the classroom...

then sail back.

At lunch there's tales of things they've seen.

That mermaid looked quite like Molene.

And Rokko's painted something new.
"Look, Migs," he says. "It's me and you."

The story's over, that's the end.

They wave goodbye to
their new friends.

Migs says, "Mum, if it's ok,
Can I go back there every day?"

Newt

Molene

Finch

Migs

Dotty

Casey

Rokko

Casey

Dotty

Newt

Finch

Migs

Molene

Rokko